# Angie Sage

# The Lonely Puppy

Illustrated by Edward Eaves

For Thomas, Chloe and Lucy,
who all share Millie

PUFFIN BOOKS

Published by the Penguin Group
Penguin Books Ltd, 80 Strand, London WC2R 0RL, England
Penguin Putnam Inc., 375 Hudson Street, New York, New York 10014, USA
Penguin Books Australia Ltd, 250 Camberwell Road, Camberwell, Victoria 3124, Australia
Penguin Books Canada Ltd, 10 Alcorn Avenue, Toronto, Ontario, Canada M4V 3B2
Penguin Books India (P) Ltd, 11 Community Centre, Panchsheel Park, New Delhi – 110 017, India
Penguin Books (NZ) Ltd, Cnr Rosedale and Airborne Roads, Albany, Auckland, New Zealand
Penguin Books (South Africa) (Pty) Ltd, 24 Sturdee Avenue, Rosebank 2196, South Africa

Penguin Books Ltd, Registered Offices: 80 Strand, London WC2R 0RL, England

www.penguin.com

First published 2003
1 3 5 7 9 10 8 6 4 2

Text copyright © Angie Sage, 2003
Illustrations copyright © Edward Eaves, 2003
All rights reserved

Set in 15/22pt Times New Roman School book

The moral right of the author and illustrator has been asserted

Printed in China by Midas Printing Ltd

British Library Cataloguing in Publication Data
A CIP catalogue record for this book is available from the British Library

ISBN 0–141–31543–1

# Contents

# 1. Busy Bings

This is the true story of a lonely puppy, Millie Bing. Millie lived in a house with Mr Bing, Mrs Bing and Baby Bing.

The Bings were very busy. Every morning they had a busy breakfast.

Baby Bing sucked up his baby banana breakfast like a small vacuum cleaner.

Mrs Bing gulped down a bowl of cereal and packed a baby bag faster than the speed of light.

Mr Bing slurped up
his cup of coffee,
grabbed his briefcase
and threw Millie a
biscuit.

Then they
rushed out.

"Bye Millie," said
Mr and Mrs Bing.

"Ba-mee," said Baby Bing.

The door slammed and Millie was left alone. All alone in the kitchen with her biscuit.

Millie jumped up to look out of the window and watch the Bings go.

But she was too late. The busy Bings had gone.

Mille looked at her biscuit, but she didn't eat it. She didn't even sniff it. Millie didn't want her biscuit, she just wanted the Bings. But Millie knew that the Bings were out all day and all day lasted a very long time.

Where, thought Millie, do the Bings go?

# 2. Cat Flap

**M**illie gazed out of the
window at the sunny garden.
She could see all of the garden,
except for the patch behind the
compost heap at the bottom of
the garden.

Maybe, thought Millie, that was where the Bings went?

It was then that Millie had her Good Idea Number One. She would go and find the Bings behind the compost heap at the bottom of the garden.

Millie's tail wagged as she thought about how pleased the Bings would be to see her.

As soon as Millie had her Good Idea Number One she wondered why she had never thought of it before.

And then she remembered why.
She couldn't get out of the kitchen.

Millie lay down by the window
and had another think. She saw the
cat from next door jump into the
garden and go and sit under Millie's
favourite tree.

"WOOF!" barked Millie. "WOOF
WOOF WOOF!"

The cat from next door looked
up and saw Millie in the window,
but she did not move. She knew that
Millie was stuck in the kitchen all
day, so she smiled a smug cat smile,
lay down on Millie's best patch of
grass and went to sleep in the sun.

It was then that Millie did
something that a dog never does.
She tried to get out through the
cat flap.

# 3. Compost Heap

**M**illie was not a big dog, but she did not look small enough to go through a cat flap.

But Millie was lonely and she had not been eating her biscuits, so now Millie was thin.

Millie pushed open the cat flap
with her nose and put her front
feet through. Then she breathed in
and pushed her tummy through.
The flap bounced along her back
until suddenly it flapped down on
her tail.

In one second,
Millie Bing was
free.

In two
seconds, the
smug cat from
next door was
back next door again.

In three seconds, Millie rushed
down to the compost heap. She
expected to find the Bings at the
bottom of the garden.

She wagged her tail and took a flying leap over the compost heap, ready to land in the Bings's arms.

Millie landed in a patch of stinging nettles. She sat up and looked around her. Her ears drooped and her tail stopped wagging.

There were no Bings at the bottom of the garden.

# 4. Outside

**M**illie Bing wandered sadly back to her tree and wondered where the Bings were.

It was then that Millie had her Good Idea Number Two. If the Bings weren't inside the garden, thought Millie, then they must be outside the garden.

So she, Millie Bing, would go outside the garden and find the Bings. Millie sat and thought about it for a bit. Outside sounded scary. But all she had to do was jump over the garden gate. Millie imagined the Bings on the other side of the gate and her tail wagged itself happily.

So Millie got up, ran as fast as she could and jumped over the garden gate. She landed with a bump on the pavement. It was harder than the

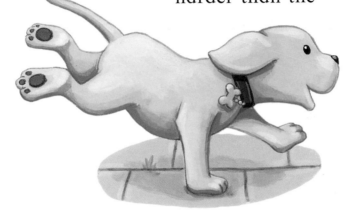

stinging nettles, but not as stingy. But when Millie looked around her, she felt just as sad as when she had sat in the stinging nettles behind the compost heap.

Because there were no Bings outside the garden either.

Millie Bing sat on the pavement and thought for a while until Good Idea Number Three arrived. Which it soon did. And it went like this:

The Bings were not inside or outside the garden. So they must be Somewhere Else.

Millie Bing stood up, wagged her tail and set off for Somewhere Else.

# 5. Somewhere Else

Millie trotted off down the street with her tail held high. She felt happy now. She was on the way to Somewhere Else. Somewhere Else where the Bings were waiting for her.

At first Millie enjoyed being out on her own. She had been out before, but only with the Bings. She always took them with her on the end of a lead and the Bings were always in a hurry, so Millie was used to walking fast and rushing past all the interesting things in the street.

But now she wandered along the street, sniffing all the sniffs and woofing at the woofs

from the other dogs in their gardens
and, most important of all, looking
for the Bings.

After a while the streets changed
to new streets where Millie and the
Bings had never been. The sniffs
were different sniffs and

the woofs
were different woofs,
and, no matter how hard Millie
looked, she could not see the Bings.

Soon Millie's paws began to feel tired. Then there were loud rumbles coming from the sky and a big drop of rain fell on to Millie's nose. Millie sat down by the side of the road and wondered what to do.

The raindrops began to fall faster. Millie's ears got wet and hung down limply.

Millie sighed. Good Idea Number Three was not working out very well. She was Somewhere Else now and the Bings were not here either.

Millie thought of Good Idea Number Four straight away. She would go home. At least she would see the Bings when they got back in the evening. But Good Idea Number Four did not last very long at all. As soon as she thought of it Millie knew it wouldn't work. Because Millie was lost.

# 6. Billy

"Look at that little dog, Mum," a voice behind Millie said.

Millie looked around and saw a boy in a blue jacket. He had curly brown hair and he was standing

beside a pushchair just like the one
Baby Bing had. Millie jumped up
excitedly, but when she saw it wasn't
Baby Bing at all, but another bigger
baby, she sat down again.

"That little dog looks sad, Mum,"
said the boy. "Can we take her home?"

"She does look rather wet," said
his mum, "but we can't take her
home. I'm sure she
belongs to
someone."

"Who?" asked
the boy.

"Have a look
on her collar,
Billy, and see
if you can find
a name or a

telephone number," said his mum.

So Billy looked
at Millie's collar.

"It says ...
M-I-L-L-I-E,"
he said slowly.
"That's
Millie. Hey,
that rhymes
with Billy.

Oh, Mum, can we take her home?
Please, please, please? Look, she's
all alone and she might run out into
the road and get squashed or
something ..."

"Oh, Billy," said Mum. "Well,
perhaps we'd better wait with
her and see if her owners come
for her."

So Billy, his mum and the bigger
baby in the pushchair stood with
Millie under Mum's umbrella in the
rain and waited for Millie's owners.

But they didn't come.

# 7. Billy's House

It was only when the rain had made everybody very wet indeed and the bigger baby in the pushchair started crying that Billy's mum said, "OK, Billy, let's take Millie home. I think she may be lost."

And Billy said, "YAY! Come on, Millie. Come home with us!"

So Millie followed Billy all the way to Billy's house. Millie liked Billy. She thought he was almost as good as a Bing.

When they got inside Billy's mum found a towel and rubbed Millie dry,

then she sat Billy and Millie down
by the fire while she put the bigger
baby (whose name was Jessy) to bed
for a sleep.

Billy put his arm round Millie and
gave her a big hug. Millie wagged
her tail and snuggled up against
Billy. Then she laid her head on his
knee and suddenly felt very tired. It
had been a long
morning and
she had had
too many
Good Ideas
for a small
dog

and had walked too far for her paws. Millie yawned and fell fast asleep. Billy ruffled her ears and read his book.

Millie was so tired that she never felt Billy's mum looking at the Bings's telephone number on her collar.

She didn't hear Billy's mum ring the number and say, "They're out. Bother. Oh it's the answer machine. Er ... um ... Oh hello,

Mr and Mrs Bing. This is Annie
Shepherd here. We found your little
dog, Millie, in our street. If you'd
like to collect her, the address is –"

"Don't tell them, Mum," yelled
Billy. "She can stay here."

"Don't be silly, Billy. The address
is ten Dove Street. Er ... bye then."

"Oh Mu-um," moaned Billy.

"Well, you can look after her until
they come to get her.

I expect they must be
really worried."

"Yeah," sighed
Billy. "I bet they
come straight
round."

But they
didn't.

# 8. Dog Food

Millie woke up when she heard the two magic words – dog food.

"I got a tin of dog food from next door," said Billy's mum. "So now we can all have lunch."

Millie followed Billy into the
kitchen. There was a small blue
bowl on the floor next to the table
with something in it that Millie
thought smelled rather
wonderful. Suddenly she was
very hungry,

and she gulped it down in less time
than it had taken her to get out
through the cat flap.

Billy's mum looked pleased. "I
thought she seemed thin. I could feel
her little ribs when I stroked her.
Maybe her owners don't feed her
properly."

"Thar or-all, um,"
said Billy with his
mouth full of
chips and beans.

"Billy, don't
talk with your
mouth full."

Billy
swallowed and
said, "That's
awful, Mum."

Baby Jessy giggled and pointed at Millie, then she dropped her biggest chip on the floor.

Millie looked at the chip. She was still a bit hungry, but she was never allowed to eat Baby Bing's food when it fell on the floor, so she just sat by the empty dog bowl.

"What a good dog you are, Millie,"

said Billy's mum as she threw the chip in the bin. "She's been well trained, you can tell that, Billy."

"She's the best," said Billy. "Can we take her to the park if the Bings don't come?"

"Let's give them a bit more time to get here, Billy. We'll go if they don't come soon."

But the Bings did not come soon. So Milly went to the park.

# 9. Orange Ball

The park was big. Much bigger than the Bings's garden. It was crammed full of interesting sniffs and happy woofs and, best of all, Billy was there with a bright orange ball for Millie to play with.

It was the best kind of game
Millie had ever played and it went
like this: Billy threw the orange ball
and Millie chased it, caught it, gave
it a good shake and brought it back
to Billy. Then Billy laughed and
ruffled Millie's ears and she dropped
the ball at his feet.

And then Billy threw the
orange ball again and
Millie chased it, caught it ...

You can guess the
rest ... Over and
over again, until
Billy's mum took
Jessy out of the
baby swings and
said that maybe
they should be

37

getting home now.

"Just one more throw, Mum,"
said Billy and he threw the orange
ball as hard as he could. He threw it
so hard that it landed in the middle
of a big clump of bushes.

But Millie didn't care. She shot off down the hill and into the bushes while Billy waited for her.

"Really, Billy," said his mum. "You didn't have to throw the ball quite so hard."

"But Millie likes it when I do," said Billy. "And I won't be able to play with her ever again."

He kicked his foot against the grass crossly while they waited for Millie to come back with the ball.

Millie pushed her way out of the bush and walked slowly back up the hill with Billy's orange ball.

Something about the way Billy was standing made her feel sad. And as Millie followed Billy back home, she kept on feeling sad.

So she just looked at the pavement and followed Billy's feet.

It was only when they reached Billy's gate that Millie looked up. And then she saw something that she had almost forgotten about, something that should have made her feel really happy.

Millie saw the Bings.

# 10. The Bings and Billy

**M**illie couldn't help it, her tail wagged itself faster than it had ever wagged before.

"Hello, Millie," said Mrs Bing, stroking Millie's ears.

"What have you been up to Millie?"

asked Mr Bing, smiling.

"Me-eee!" squeaked Baby Bing, laughing.

"Oh," said Billy.

"Hello," Mrs Bing said to Billy's mum. "I'm Audrey Bing and this is my husband, Bernard Bing. Thank you so much for finding Millie for us."

"And for looking after her. I do hope she hasn't been too much trouble," finished Bernard Bing.

"Millie's lovely," said Billy, staring crossly at the Bings. "She's not trouble."

"Well, er ..." said Billy's mum, "perhaps you'd like to come in for a cup of tea so that Billy can –"

"Thanks, but we must rush," said Audrey Bing.

"We're running a bit late tonight, what with finding Millie gone," said Bernard Bing. "Traffic was terrible. Must be off, but thank you so much."

And with that he scooped Millie up and put her in the car.

Just before the car door closed
Billy threw the orange ball to
Millie. She caught it and held it in
her mouth.

"It's for you, Millie. Bye!"
shouted Billy as Audrey Bing
jumped into the driver's seat,

started the engine and zoomed off.

"Millie's gone," said Billy.

"I know, love," said his mum and she gave him a big hug.

# 11. Dog Basket

W hen Millie arrived home the Bings gave her a special biscuit as a treat. They made a big fuss of her. Mrs Bing brushed her coat and Mr Bing gave Millie her favourite dog food for supper.

But all Millie really wanted to do was to sit in her dog basket.

So that's what Millie did. She sat in her dog basket and she thought. Millie thought that she felt happy and sad at the same time. The being-back-with-the-Bings-bit felt happy, but the leaving-Billy-bit felt sad. Really sad.

After supper Millie watched Bernard Bing nail the cat flap closed.

Then the Bings went upstairs to
watch television. Millie usually went
with them, but somehow that
evening she didn't want to.

She just snuggled down in her dog
basket with her orange ball and fell
fast asleep.

Later that evening the telephone
rang, but Millie didn't hear it. She
was fast asleep, busy dreaming
about playing with Billy in the park.

# 12. The Car

The next morning Millie woke up
in her dog basket and watched
the busy Bings

They had a busy breakfast.

Baby Bing sucked up his baby
banana breakfast like a small

vacuum cleaner.

Mrs Bing gulped down a bowl of cereal and packed a baby bag faster than the speed of light.

Mr Bing slurped up his cup of coffee, grabbed his briefcase and threw Millie a biscuit. Then they rushed out.

And then ... they rushed back in again.

"Oops, nearly forgot," said Mr Bing.

He scooped Millie up and ran down
the garden path with Millie under
one arm and his briefcase under the
other.

Mrs Bing was waiting for them
in the car.

Millie sat on the back seat next to
Baby Bing while they waited in the
road with a lot of other cars.

Every now and then the Bings's car moved a little bit.

So this is what the Bings do, thought Millie. They sit in their car all day. No wonder I couldn't find them yesterday.

Millie liked sitting in the car. She liked listening to the radio and she liked eating the rusk that Baby Bing gave her.

After a while the car stopped by a garden gate that Millie had seen before. Mr Bing lifted Millie out.

Someone was waiting for her.

# 13. The Shared Puppy

It was Billy!
"Millie!"
yelled Billy.

"Woof!" woofed Millie.

Mr Bing rushed up to Billy
and put Millie into his arms,

then he jumped back into the car.

"Bye, Millie," called Mr and Mrs
Bing, waving.

"Ba-mee," gurgled Baby Bing.

The car door slammed and Millie
was left – but this time she wasn't
alone. This time she was with Billy.

Billy's mum came out and waved

goodbye to the Bings.

"See you this evening," she shouted.

"Yes. Must rush!" shouted the busy Bings as their car sped away.

"Do we really have Millie all day, Mum?" asked Billy.

"All day, Billy. All day and every day while Mr and Mrs Bing are at work, we are going to look after Millie, aren't we, Millie?"

"Woof!" woofed Millie.

And that is the true story of Millie Bing, the shared puppy.